CONTENTS

The Seasons in Fern Hollow

Spring in Fern Hollow

In Fern Hollow, as in other places, Spring is
a time of great activity; a time for gardening,
for whitewashing and for Spring cleaning.

It is a restless time of year when no-one can stand still for very long, but after chatting to you for a minute or two they will mumble, "I really must get that door painted," or "Dear me, it's May already, and I haven't planted my vegetables yet," and off they will rush to get things done!

It was Easter time and
Monty was helping his
Father, Mr. Tuttleebee, to
repair the roof, while Spud
and Heather played with
their Easter eggs.

In the shop Mrs. Tuttleebee
was wrapping some Spring flowers
for Mr. Willowbank.
"They will be a nice surprise Easter
present for Mrs. Willowbank," said the
Hedgehog.

It was such a beautiful Spring day, and it seemed so stuffy inside the old school house that Miss Crisp decided to take her class out of doors.

The lesson was in arithmetic, which was usually rather boring (to everyone except Clarence Hoppit, who was clever at that sort of thing), but today, in the fresh air, arithmetic didn't seem too bad at all!

It was a fine day for the Spring Jumble Sale in the Vicarage gardens, and Parson Dimly, who was looking after the Lucky Dip, was pleased to see that lots of animals had turned up.

Mrs. Dimly took care of the refreshments,
while Lupin had lots of fun on the Jumble
Stall, which was filled with clothes the Fern
Hollow animals had cleared out during
their Spring cleaning.

Constable Hoppit was taking a walk with
his family on his day off work, when they
were caught in an April shower! Clarence
and Clarissa hurried along with their
Mother, while Constable Hoppit picked up
little Horace and raced on in front.

Then, under the shelter of the beech trees,
they all watched the rainbow while they got
their breath back, and waited for the rain
to stop.

In Boris Blink's Antiquarian Bookshop,
Boris and his assistant Leapy were Spring
cleaning, when professor Sigmund Swamp
dropped in, looking for a book on Famous
Toads.

"I think you will find one in that pile over there," said Boris.

"Dear me!" exclaimed the professor. "It would be like looking for a needle in a haystack. I think I'd better come back tomorrow when you've got the books back on the shelves again."

Mr. and Mrs. Rusty had taken their cubs, Dusty, Rufus and Redvers out to fly a kite in the March winds. Rufus held onto the line, while Redvers chased around trying to catch the kite's tail, but soon it was flying so far out of reach that it was almost touching the clouds.

Summer
in
Fern Hollow

Everyone in Fern Hollow looks forward to
the Summer, to the lovely days spent
picnicking by the River Ferny and to the
visits to the seaside.

On their long summer holidays from
school, the little animals go swimming and
fishing, or play hide and seek in Windy
Wood.

The bumble bees bumble around amongst the wild flowers, dragonflies zoom low over the river and no-one feels very much like work, though of course there is still plenty to be done!

Mr. Bramble the Farmer was in the middle of haymaking. The hay had already been baled and now Tugger and Madge were helping to load it onto the trailer. Little Tuppence was too small to help, but she had a cumfy ride on top of the hay.

In the middle of the afternoon, Mrs. Bramble arrived with lots of lovely things to eat and drink. Then the busy badgers stopped work for a picnic.

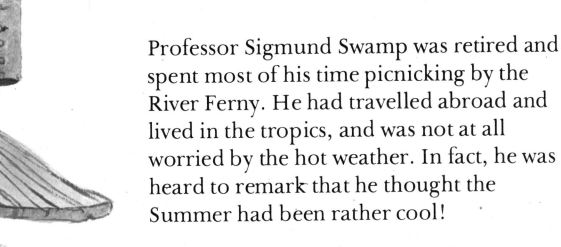

Professor Sigmund Swamp was retired and spent most of his time picnicking by the River Ferny. He had travelled abroad and lived in the tropics, and was not at all worried by the hot weather. In fact, he was heard to remark that he thought the Summer had been rather cool!

Mr. Twinkle's family were spending a lovely Summer's afternoon by the pool in the garden. Mrs. Twinkle was relaxing under the shade of a mushroom, while Mr. Twinkle floated pleasantly around the pool on an airbed.

Sparky, Dash and Skipper played around on the springboard, and Midge practised her diving.

The Summer was so hot that the River Ferny had dried up, and there wasn't enough water to turn Mr. Croaker's mill wheel.

"Never mind," said Mrs. Croaker. "We can all take a holiday until the rain begins to fall again."
"Hooray!" cried Lily. "Can we go to the seaside?"
"Yes, of course," chuckled Mr. Croaker.
"And Dipper can sail his yacht in the sea!"

At the Railway Station Mr. Twinkle was having trouble with some foreign visitors who had lost their tickets. Fortunately the problem was soon solved by old Stripey, the Porter, who found them lying on the platform.

Meanwhile Mr. Rusty, the Engine Driver,
checked his wrist watch with Mr. Prickles'
and blew the Bluebell's whistle to warn the
passengers that it was time to leave.

At the Jolly Vole Hotel, Mrs. Crackleberry
and Poppy were serving cold drinks and ice
creams to the guests at the outside tables,
when Jingle's taxi arrived with the foreign
visitors. Mr. Crackleberry picked up the
Raccoon family's luggage and led them off
to their room. Unfortunately no one had
remembered to pay Jingle!

Autumn
in
Fern Hollow

Autumn is a beautiful time of year in Fern Hollow. The trees of Windy Wood turn golden, red and orange, and there is a wonderful scent in the air.

Unfortunately, the fallen leaves do cause
the animals something of a problem,
because they all like to keep their gardens
tidy. Of course you can always make a little
bonfire of the leaves, but it is best to check
which way the wind is blowing first!

Mr. Prickles had taken a day off from his job as a guardsman at Fern Hollow railway station, to gather the fruit and nuts in Windy Wood. The expedition had been very successful and, with the help of Mrs. Prickles and Polly, Mr. Prickles had managed to fill his cart so well that there was hardly room for another acorn!

Jasper, Patch, Tugger and
Monty decided it would be
fun to raid an orchard.
Unfortunately for them
P.C. Hoppit came by on his
bicycle and caught them—all
except for Jasper the squirrel,
who was very quick at
climbing up and down trees,
and managed to run away.

Dilly and Pud's Hallowe'en costumes were the best in the village. This was hardly surprising as their parents, Mr. and Mrs. Thimble, were the Fern Hollow tailors.

Dilly and Pud's friends were dressed in pixie or goblin costumes and some of them wore masks so that you couldn't tell who they were!

In the heart of Windy Wood Mr. Chips and his sons
Chucky and Flip were cutting down trees and chopping
them up for firewood in preparation for the Winter.

The hard work had made them feel very hungry and they
were all pleased when Mrs. Chips shouted that the soup
was ready.

One gusty day in October Lord Trundle was taking a stroll around the grounds at Trundleberry Manor when he bumped into old Blodger, his gardener, who was having trouble with the fallen leaves. Every time Blodger swept them into a neat little pile, the wind came along and blew them away again!

Mrs. Bouncer poked the baked potatoes
out of the bonfire and handed them round
to the children.
"One for Patch, one for Pippa and one
for little Toby," she said. "Be
careful, they are rather hot."

Mr. Bouncer lit a sky rocket
and it flew high up into the
night sky.
"Good gracious," laughed
Grandpa Bobber. "It looks
like it's going all the way to the
moon!"

Winter
in
Fern Hollow

Winter in Fern Hollow is more often
than not very cold with plenty of snow.
This suits some of the little animals very
well. They can build snowmen, sledge
and skate on the River Ferny.

But not everyone likes that sort of thing,
and some say that there is nothing
better than gathering a great big stack
of wood, making a nice warm fire and
maybe toasting a few crumpets.

Mr. Willowbank was a marvellous cobbler and could usually mend an old shoe so that you wouldn't have known it from a new one. But when Spike brought him Mr. Bouncer's Fireman's boots, he shook his head and said they would have to be thrown away.

"How on earth did your boots get such enormous holes in them?" asked Mrs. Willowbank.

"I put them by the fireside to dry," admitted Mr. Bouncer, "and they burnt."

"That was a silly thing for a Fireman to do," laughed Spike.

Jasper and Podger bustled excitedly into Brock Gruffy's shop. They had just emptied their Piggy banks and found that they might possibly have enough money to buy a sledge. Mr. Gruffy was very helpful and managed to find a super sledge at about the right price. Actually, it cost a bit more than the two little squirrels had managed to save, but the kind old Badger said that, seeing as it was them, they could have it anyway!

Mrs. Periwinkle could hardly believe
her eyes; Mr. Periwinkle had forgotten
to buckle up his postbag and all the
Trundleberry Manor Christmas Party
invitations were blowing away.

Fortunately Wally managed to catch up
with the bicycle and Mr. Periwinkle
came back to gather up the invitations.
"I hope I haven't lost any of them," he
worried.
"No one wants to be left out of the
Party I'm sure!"

Fergus was all tucked up in bed suffering from a terrible cold.

"Not to worry," said his Father, Dr. Bushy.

"We'll give you some medicine and you'll be right as rain in no time."

"Yes, we must get you well quickly Fergus," said
Mrs. Bushy, "The Trundleberry Manor Party is only a
few days away!"

In the bakery Mr. Acorn was busy baking lots of delicious things to eat for the Christmas party. Jiggy watched her Mother icing a cake, while Jasper did his best to help by fetching and carrying. As for little Podger, it was long past his bedtime and he had fallen asleep on the floor!

And then at last it was Christmas Day, and time for the Trundleberry Manor Christmas Party! Everyone turned up (obviously Mr. Periwinkle, the Postman, hadn't managed to lose any of the invitations), and they all agreed that it was the best Christmas party there ever was!

SPORTS DAY

It was still very early in the morning,
but some of the Fern Hollow animals
were already busily preparing for
the Sports Day, which, as usual, was to
be held in one of Farmer Bramble's
fields. Spike and Patch had been
given the job of painting the white
lines for the running lanes.

Meanwhile,
on the edge of the
field, Mr. Chips whistled happily
to himself as he went about the business of
putting up a refreshments stand.
"It's beginning to look quite splendid, Mr. Chips,"
exclaimed Mr. Acorn, who was supplying the cakes and buns.
"It certainly is," agreed Mr. Crackleberry, rolling a big
barrel of orange juice off the back of his wagon.
"I hope the weather stays fine though—there's a big
black cloud over there on the horizon."

At Trundleberry Manor, Lord Trundle packed the sports day prizes into a trunk and carried them out to his car. He too noticed the dark cloud on the horizon, but he was in too much of a hurry to give it much thought and, jumping into the car, he drove off to the sports field.

Suddenly, as he was driving over the bridge by the Jolly Vole Hotel, Lord Trundle's car hit a big stone lying in the road.

It was such a hard bump
that the trunk containing
the prizes shot off the roof
rack and with a great
SPLOSH!
landed in the River Ferny.

Luckily the trunk floated, but it was soon caught in the
current and swept away down the river.
"Oh no!" panted Lord Trundle,
rushing along the river bank.
"What ever shall we do?"

The Sports Day prizes would certainly have been lost if it had not been for Sigmund Swamp, who was out fishing, and seeing the trunk floating by, cast out his line and caught it, just as if it had been a great big fish!

It turned out that Sigmund had quite forgotten that it was the Sports Day, and was very pleased when Lord Trundle offered him a lift in his car. By the time they arrived at the sports field, the tug of war was about to begin, but the big black cloud was now directly overhead.

Each of the two teams led by P.C. Hoppit and Brock Gruffy got a firm grip on the rope. Boris Blink slowly raised the starting pistol and — BANG — the contest began.

A few moments later the big black cloud burst.
The rain came pouring down and, in next to no
time, the field became waterlogged.
The tug of war teams slipped and slid around
in the mud, fell into the puddles and looked
quite ridiculous.

Everyone ran for the shelter of the
trees or the refreshments stand,
where they all stood around looking
very glum. It looked as if the Sports
Day would have to be cancelled.
The sky was now completely covered
with clouds and the rain was falling
harder all the time!

Then Lord Trundle had a wonderful idea.
"Everyone is invited to Trundleberry Manor," he cried.
"We'll hold the Sports Day indoors!"
All the animals agreed that it was a fine idea and they
quickly made their way to the Manor.

The sack race was held in the great hall, and was won by Dipper Croaker, who, being a frog, could hop further and faster than anyone, even in a sack!

The egg and spoon race up and down the main staircase was great fun. Clarence Hoppit was in the lead for most of the way, but he dropped his egg and Dusty Rusty won by a whisker.

Then came the special event, the bannister slide. The contestants slid down the bannister, flew off the end, and landed on a mattress. Spike Willowbank won this quite easily, but he overshot the mattress and landed on top of Brock Gruffy!

When the games were all over, Sigmund Swamp set up
his camera to take a picture of the prize giving ceremony.
"Smile everyone," said Sigmund.

Everyone did smile and it made a marvellous picture!

PARSON DIMLY'S
TREASURE HUNT

It was Sunday and Parson Dimly was busy in the church laying out the hymn books for the morning service. As he bustled around he sang to himself, "all things bright and beautiful." Suddenly another voice joined in.

"Chirp, chirp, chirp." The old mole looked up and saw a little sparrow. It had flown in through a large hole in the church roof.

"Good gracious," the parson exclaimed. "That hole must have been caused by the storm we had last night. I must get it fixed at once, but how on earth can I raise the funds?"

After giving the matter some thought, Parson Dimly decided to raise the money to mend the roof by holding a treasure hunt. The Fern Hollow animals all bought tickets and turned up with all kinds of vehicles. There were cars, motorcycles, a tandem, the fire engine and Sigmund Swamp on his penny farthing. In fact, the only animal who arrived on foot was Polly Prickles. Poor Polly — no-one thought she stood the slightest chance of winning the race to the treasure.

Now it was time to begin the treasure hunt by reading the first clue.

"Look in a tree, in a little round hole
which stands in a place by a happy old vole,"
read Parson Dimly.

Brock Gruffy realised at once what the clue referred to and quickly drove off to the Jolly Vole Hotel, where he jumped

out of his car and ran down to the river bank to the hollow tree. Unfortunately poor Brock forgot to put the car's handbrake on and his car rolled down the bank after him, and with a great splash, ended up in the river!

The next animal to arrive at the hollow tree was Sigmund Swamp. Sigmund read the clue —
Now you're wondering what to do
Where the river is crossed you'll find the next clue.
"That must mean Ferny Bank Ferry," said the clever toad to himself. and away he went, pedalling furiously.

When Sigmund reached the ferry he rode out onto the jetty
to the signpost where he could see a piece of paper had been
pinned. Suddenly there was a loud bang and Sigmund fell off
his penny farthing. The poor toad had ridden over a nail and
punctured a tyre.

The clue pinned to the signpost at the Ferry read —
        The third clue you will find today
        Is where the farmer stores his hay.
It was easy to guess that this must mean Farmer Bramble's
barn, and very soon the farm yard and the barn were
crammed with traffic. Everyone had read the clue which was
pinned to the barn door, but they had got themselves into
such a jam that no-one could get out!

Eventually Polly Prickles arrived
at the barn. She was feeling
rather tired because of course she
had had to run all the way —
"To find the treasure run as fast
as you can
Back to the place where the hunt
began,"
puffed Polly, reading the clue on
the barn door. Then away
she ran as fast as she could back
to the vicarage garden.

In the garden Polly found a huge hamper of food and a trophy with "Winner of the Grand Treasure Hunt" inscribed on it. Perhaps this wasn't real treasure, but it had all been great fun and Polly decided to share the hamper with all the other contestants and Parson Dimly, so they all had a lovely picnic.

The next day Parson Dimly counted the money which the treasure hunt had raised, and was pleased to find that it easily covered the cost of mending the church roof. Naturally, the work was done by Mr Chips and his sons, Chucky and Flip, who made a very good job of it.

THE UNSCARY SCARECROW

Farmer Bramble had woken up bright and early. He had a very busy day in front of him, and as usual he and his family were tucking into a hearty breakfast.

"Cock a doodle-do, cock a doodle-do," crowed Farmer Bramble's cockerel, flying up onto the kitchen window sill.

"You're late again, cockerel" chuckled Farmer Bramble. "It's a good thing I've got a proper alarm clock to wake me up in the morning — you're certainly not an early riser!"

After his breakfast, feeling very happy, Farmer Bramble
went out to begin his day's work. He was singing a little
song —
"Fern Hollow is the place to be
The leaves are green on every tree
The sky is blue, don't need a brolly
And I'm a farmer, round and jolly."

The little song came to an abrupt end as Farmer Bramble
noticed a flock of big black crows in his field, all greedily
gobbling up the wheat.

"Be off with you," shouted the angry badger, rushing
around the field and waving his arms about. "Leave my
wheat alone!"

But the poor old farmer, being rather too fat, soon grew
tired and had to stop for breath. Then the cheeky crows
settled down again to eating his crop.

Mrs Bramble decided that the best thing to do was to build a scarecrow. Of course the three children were happy to help. It was all great fun. A turnip was used for the scarecrow's head and his old clothes were stuffed with hay and tied with string. He looked really marvellous. But when he was put in the field, the crows sat on his hat and arms and carried on eating the wheat. The scarecrow just wasn't very scary!

When Mr Periwinkle the postman arrived with Mr Bramble's letters, he suggested that the scarecrow might be more effective if he had a scary face.

"That's a good idea," agreed Mr Bramble. "I've got some cans of paint and a brush. Perhaps you would like to paint the scarecrow's face on for me, Mr Periwinkle."

The postman was a keen amateur artist, and was really
rather pleased to show off his abilities. The job only took five
minutes and everyone admitted that the face was very scary
indeed. But the cheeky crows took no notice of it at all, and
continued eating Farmer Bramble's wheat!

As the Brambles stood wondering what on earth they could do to get rid of the pesky crows, the Fern Hollow express passed by, and Mr Rusty the engine driver gave the farmers a friendly wave and sounded the train's whistle.

Toot, toot. Toot, toot, went the train whistle loudly, and all the crows flew up into the air. The whistle had frightened them away, but soon they came back again and began, once more, to gobble up the wheat. Then Mr Bramble rubbed his chin and smiled.

"I've had an idea," he said to his wife.

Wasting no time, Farmer Bramble drove his tractor round to the railway station, where he went to see his friend the engine driver. Mr Rusty was in the engine shed polishing up the brass fittings on the train.

"Hello there Farmer Bramble," he said cheerily. "What can I do for you?"

"Well I was wondering if you had an old train whistle you could let me have," replied the badger.

"I should think so," said Mr Rusty helpfully, fishing around in a pile of bits and pieces. "Yes, here's one."

Farmer Bramble thanked his friend profusely and drove off on his tractor.

"I wonder what he is going to do with an old train whistle," mumbled Mr Rusty, scratching his head.

Back at the farm, the clever badger began building a peculiar machine. It was made up of all kinds of odd things; an alarm clock, an old car engine, bits of string, levers and pulleys, and most important of all, the engine whistle. When it was finally completed the farmer filled his machine with petrol and, with the help of Tugger, carried it out into the wheat field and stood it by the side of the scarecrow. All the crows in the field stopped eating and eyed the machine suspiciously.

"Stand back everyone," cried Farmer Bramble, and he
pulled hard on the starting cord.

Chug, chug, chug, went the machine, and for a while that's
all it did. Then, quite suddenly, it blew the old engine
whistle.

Toot, toot. Toot, toot.

It sounded just like the Fern Hollow express, and the greedy
crows were so frightened that they all flew away. To make
sure that the pests did not come back, farmer Bramble had
designed his machine to blow the whistle automatically every
ten minutes.

"Hip hip hooray, the crows have gone away!" shouted
Tugger, and everyone laughed. As for the unscary scarecrow
— he never said a word!

THE BRASS BAND ROBBERY

One morning a large wooden crate arrived on the goods train at Fern Hollow station. It was addressed to Lord Trundle and marked "FRAGILE".
"I wonder what it can be?" said old Stripey, the Porter.
"I don't know," replied Mr. Twinkle, the Station Master. "But I'd better telephone Lord Trundle to let him know it's arrived."

When he heard the news, Lord Trundle was very excited and rushed down to the railway station in his car. "Ah, at last!" he cried, looking at the great big wooden crate. "I've been waiting for this to arrive for weeks."

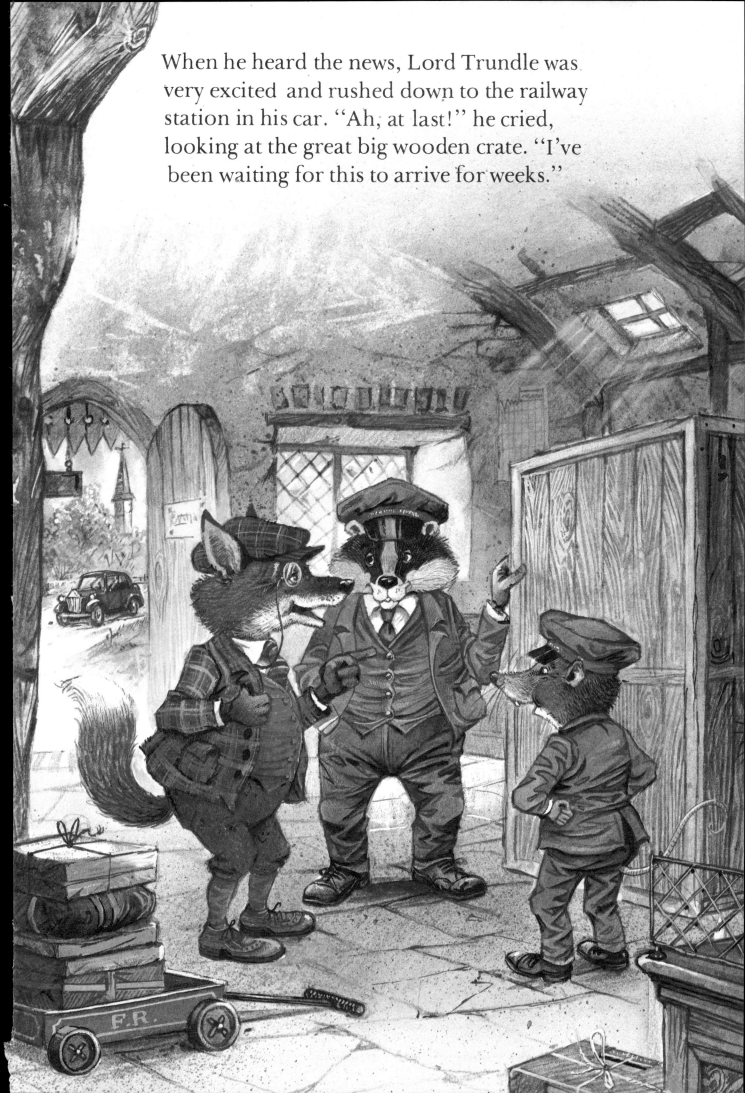

The crate was much too big to go inside Lord Trundle's car, so old Stripey and Mr. Twinkle helped him to tie it on to the roof rack, then away went the car, bouncing and rattling down the road.

The next day
Lord Trundle held
a meeting at Trundleberry Manor.
"As you all know," he began, "May Day isn't far away
now, and I wanted to do something really special in the
way of celebrations, so I've bought these!"
Lord Trundle pointed to the great big wooden crate.
"Musical instruments," he went on. "Fern Hollow is
going to have a brass band!"

Everyone had been given a musical instrument and the band had begun to practise, when suddenly the door burst open and in walked Snitch and Snatch. No one had invited them because they were always causing trouble. The two sneaky weasles had been peeping through the keyhole and had decided that they wanted to join the band.

"Give me the big drum," said Snatch.

"I'll have the sousaphone," said Snitch.

"I'm afraid there are only two triangles left," said Lord
Trundle politely.

"We don't want your silly triangles!" screamed Snitch.

"And what's more, if we can't have the drum and
sousaphone, then you won't have them for long either!"
And off they went, slamming the door behind them.

That night, Snitch and Snatch broke into Trundleberry
Manor intending to steal the drum and sousaphone. But as
Snitch was carrying the drum down the steps in front of
the Manor, it slipped out of his hands.
BOOM BOOM BOOM
 it went as it bounced down the steps.

The noise woke Lord Trundle, who jumped out of bed and looked out of his window, just in time to see the two weasles running away with the musical instruments. Quickly Lord Trundle telephoned Fern Hollow Police Station.

Constable Hoppit arrived a few minutes later, looking slightly out of breath from pedalling his bicycle so fast. "Don't worry, Lord Trundle," he panted. "We'll soon track the villains down. Which way did they go?"

Lord Trundle pointed
out the direction which
Snitch and Snatch had taken,
and followed P.C. Hoppit as the
Policeman raced off in pursuit.

"There they are," cried P.C. Hoppit. "Down on the river bank. We've got them now—they'll never be able to swim all the way across the Ferny with the drum and sousaphone!"

But the wily weasles had a plan. They
pushed the big drum out into the river
and jumped on top. Then Snitch began
to paddle with a stick, while Snatch held
onto the sousaphone.

Soon the weasles were halfway across
the river leaving Lord Trundle and P.C.
Hoppit standing helplessly on the bank.

It looked very much like Snitch and Snatch were going to get away, but suddenly the drum became caught in a strong current, and was swept away down river.

The terrified weasles clung onto the drum for all they were worth, but it was no use, because they were quickly swept over the waterfalls. Luckily for them, Mr. Whirlygill, the Ferryman, was watching and was able to drag them both out.

As a punishment P.C. Hoppit locked
Snitch and Snatch up in Fern Hollow
Police Station for a few days where they
missed all the May Day fun.
Lord Trundle's brass band was, of course,
a great success. They paraded around the
streets of Fern Hollow all afternoon,
before at last they stopped for a well-
deserved rest at the Jolly Vole,
where Mr. Crackleberry supplied
everyone with orange juice
and sandwiches!

Fern Hollow

MR. CHIPS'S HOUSE

MR. WILLOWBANK'S
COBBLER'S SHOP

MR. CROAKER'S WATERMILL

STRIPEY'S HOUSE

SCHOOL

THE JOLLY VOLE
HOTEL

RIVER FERNY

MR. ACORN'S
BAKERY

MR. RUSTY'S HOUSE

MR. PRICKLES'S HOUSE

POST OFFICE

BORIS BLINKS'S
BOOKSHOP

MR. TWINKLE'S
HOUSE

MR. TUTTLEEBEE'S
SHOP

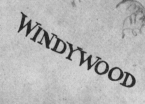

MR. THIMBLE'S
TAILOR'S SHOP

WINDYWOOD